Tulsa and the Frog

There are lots of Early Reader stories
you might enjoy.

Look at the back of the book or,
for a complete list, visit
www.orionbooks.co.uk

Tulsa and the Frog

Written and illustrated by
Tony Ross

Orion
Children's Books

First published in Great Britain in 2013
by Orion Children's Books
a division of the Orion Publishing Group Ltd
Orion House
5 Upper Saint Martin's Lane
London WC2H 9EA
An Hachette UK Company

1 3 5 7 9 10 8 6 4 2

The Orion Publishing Group's policy is to use papers that are natural,
renewable and recyclable products and made from wood grown in
sustainable forests. The logging and manufacturing processes are expected
to conform to the environmental regulations of the country of origin.

ISBN 978 1 4440 0927 9

A catalogue record for this book is available from the British Library.

Printed in China

www.orionbooks.co.uk

Tulsa was a **silly** name.

Worse than that, it was a
horrible name.

Worse than that, Tulsa hated
being called Tulsa.

Worse than that, her second name was not much better.

She was called Tulsa Pomfret. Honestly, **Tulsa Pomfret**, even the dog laughed.

Sometimes, the other children
called her Pom Pom Pomfret.

That was bad, but better than Tulsa. Tulsa hated her name so much, she wanted to be someone else.

Anybody else would do, so
Tulsa imagined that she was some
of the people who lived in her
story books.

This is how it worked. When Tulsa was reading Snow White and The Seven Dwarves, she became Snowy and The Seven Dolls.

She would pretend that her
seven dolls were doing all the work
that Snow White had to do.

She had more than seven dolls really, but only needed seven for this game.

19

When Mum called, "Tulsa, time for tea," she didn't hear.

When Mum called "Snowy, time for tea," she said goodbye to the seven dolls, and went downstairs.

Tulsa had some teddy bears.
She picked the biggest one, and
the next to biggest one, and the
smallest one. Of course, she
became Goldilocks.

The best bit about being
Goldilocks, was having three bowls
of porridge for breakfast, and
being called Goldy.

When Dad found her in his
bed, he said, "Tulsa, what are you
doing in my bed?"

Tulsa didn't say anything, so Dad said, "Goldy, what are you doing in my bed?"

"Just trying it out, but it's horribly hard," she said, jumping to the floor.

When Tulsa read Pippi
Longstocking, she wore one black
stocking and one brown one.

She put her hair into plaits, and hung upside down in the apple tree, pretending to be in Sweden.

"Tulsa," called Mum . . .

"I'm not Tulsa, I'm Pippi!"

"Pippi!" said Mum. "What would you like for your birthday?"

"I want a big horse, a small monkey with a hat, and a Swedish dictionary," replied Tulsa.

When her birthday arrived, she got a toy monkey without a hat.

No big horse, and no Swedish dictionary.

Tulsa made a hat for the monkey.

"You can be called Mr Nelson," she told the monkey.

Without the dictionary, it
wasn't easy to speak Swedish,
so Tulsa stopped being Pippi
Longstocking, and went back to
her story books.

She was in her bedroom,
reading Rapunzel, when she heard
someone calling "Tulsa . . ."

It was Next Door Daniel.

"I'm not Tulsa!" she shouted,
"I am Rapa."

"OK, Rapa," replied Daniel.
"Coming out to play?"

Tulsa thought about Rapunzel
for a moment.

"No," she called. "You can come up here, I'll let down my hair. You can climb up my hair, and meet me in my tower."

She hung her hair out of the window. (It wasn't in plaits now.)

Daniel jumped and jumped, but he could not reach Rapa's hair.

It was not as long as it was in the book. Less than twenty centimetres, in fact.

"I'll come back tomorrow, when it's longer," said Daniel.

Tulsa went back to her books. There were lots of people she would rather be than Tulsa. Some of them were poor girls with names like Cinders. Cindy would be OK, she thought.

But most of them were
princesses.

If I was a princess, she thought,
my name would be **Your
Majesty**. That's much better
than Tulsa!

So she made herself a crown,
and set off looking for adventure.

"Where are you off to Pippi?"
asked Mum.

"I'm not Pippi, I am Your
Majesty," she answered in a royal
sort of voice. "And I am going for a
walk in the enchanted forest."

The enchanted forest was the
bit of woodland between her back
garden and the supermarket.
There was an enchanted pond in
the middle of it.

"Help!" A shrill voice came from the enchanted pond.

Her Majesty stopped. She saw a frog, sitting on a leaf in the water.

"Did you say something?"

"I did," said the frog, puffing himself up to the size of an apple. "I said, help."

"I didn't know frogs could talk," said Her Majesty, shaking the water off him.

"Ahhh," replied the frog, "I'm an enchanted frog. Kiss me, and I will turn back into the handsome prince I used to be."

"Golly gosh," thought Tulsa. "I really am a fairytale princess, now I have an enchanted frog."

She put the frog into her pocket.

"Oi, kiss me!" screeched the frog.

"Not right now," said Her Majesty, thinking the frog was a bit ugly for that.

"What's that?" asked Dad when she got home.

"Nothing," said Tulsa, slapping her pocket.

"Oooh!" gasped her pocket.

Later, when Tulsa went to bed, she couldn't sleep, because of the frog shouting, **"Kiss me!"** So she stuffed her jeans into a drawer, where she couldn't hear the squeals.

Next day, Tulsa put on the same jeans.

"Oi, what about me, **kiss me**," came out of the pocket.

In the garden, the frog went on and on and on.

"I want to be a handsome prince again. Kiss me, kiss me."

"Tulsa, what's all the noise about?" shouted Next Door Daniel.

"Nothing!" said Tulsa.

She didn't even mind her silly name any more.

Not now she was a **real** enchanted princess. Not now she was special.

"Kiss me!" croaked the frog.

Tulsa dived into the shed, where nobody could see her.

She pulled the enchanted frog out of her pocket, and he sat on her hand, staring at her.

"I know I'm not in great shape right now," he said, "but I will be when I turn into a handsome prince. Why won't you kiss me?"

Tulsa had seen lots of princes in her story books, and on TV.

"Handsome princes are ten
a penny," she smiled. "I think I
would rather have a talking frog."

What are you going to read next?

More adventures with

or go to sea with

Horrid Henry,

or into space with

Poppy the Pirate Dog,

You could have fun on

Cudweed.

A Rainbow Shopping Day,

or explore

Down in the Jungle,

but watch out for

A Creepy Crawly Story!

Make magic with

The Three Little Witches,

and have
a ball
with

Princesses.

Or follow the star in

The First Christmas.

Enjoy all the Early Readers.

the
orion star

Sign up for **the orion star** newsletter
for all the latest children's book news,
plus activity sheets, exclusive competitions,
author interviews, pre-publication extracts
and more.

www.orionbooks.co.uk/newsletters

Follow  @the_orionstar on 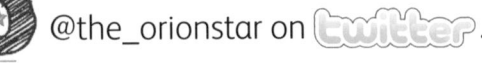 .